Pooh's Halloween Parade

Disney's
Winnie the Pooh First Readers

Disney's
A Winnie the Pooh First Reader

Pooh's Halloween Parade

Isabel Gaines
Illustrated by Ted Enik and Paul Wenzel

Random House 🏠 New York

Library of Congress Number: 00-108702
ISBN: 0-7364-1148-8 (paperback)

First Random House Edition: January 2001

www.randomhouse.com/kids/disney

Printed in the United States of America 10 9 8 7 6

Pooh's Halloween Parade

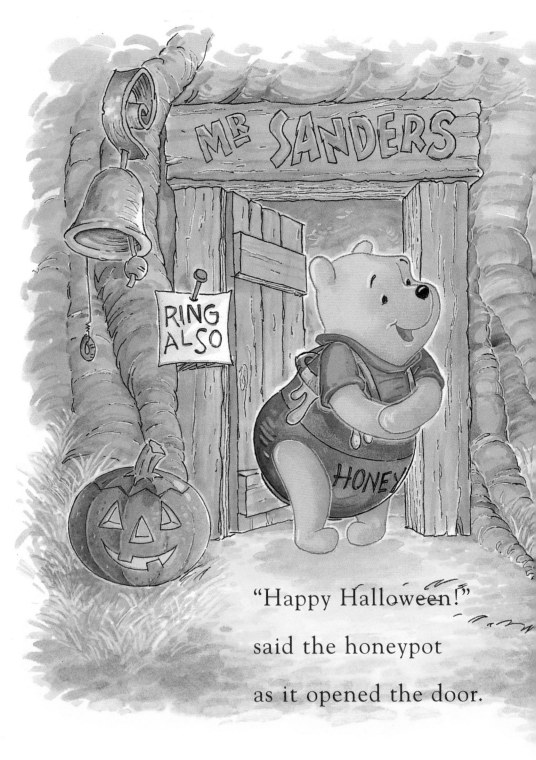

"Happy Halloween!"
said the honeypot
as it opened the door.

In came a pirate,

a rabbit with black and orange stripes,

and a forest ranger in a big hat.

The honeypot walked up
to the ranger and said,
"Hello. My name is Pooh.
Do I know you?"

"Pooh! It's me, Rabbit!"

"Oh, Rabbit!" said Pooh.

"I didn't recognize you

without your ears."

"No! *I* am Rabbit!" cried the rabbit
with the orange and black stripes.
He laughed a Tigger laugh.

"Can't be," said Rabbit.

"Rabbits do not have stripes."

11

Just then, Owl walked in.

He wore a black cap.

There was a big sign on his belly.

"Welcome, Owl!" said Pooh.

"What are you?"

"The alphabet, of course,"

said Owl.

"Wait for us!" said a nurse

as she walked in the door.

A small ghost followed her.

Then a strange thing happened.

A rock walked in by itself!

It went to the back of the room

and stood very still.

Nobody noticed it.

"It's time for the parade!" cried Roo.

"Not yet," said Pooh.

"Christopher Robin and Eeyore
are not here yet."

But then Pooh and his friends

heard strange noises

coming from the back

of the room.

They sounded like

whistle, snort, whistle, snort.

17

Everyone looked toward

the back of the room.

All they saw was a big rock.

"I've never heard a rock

go whistle, snort before,"

said Pooh.

The rock stopped going

whistle, snort

and started going zzzzz.

Then it let out a loud "Rah!"

"Oh, dear!" yelled Pooh.

Everyone ran to the front

of the room.

They huddled together,

shaking with fear.

Suddenly, there was a knock

at the door.

"Aah!" they all screamed,

and jumped straight in the air.

The door opened,

and there stood a giant bat!

Everyone hid under Pooh's table.

"Hi, everybody," said the bat.

"It's me, Christopher Robin."

"Oh, Christopher Robin," said Pooh.

"Are we glad to see you!"

"There's a big rock

in the house," said Piglet.

"It's making scary noises,"

said Roo.

"Tiggers don't like scary noises,"

said Tigger.

Christopher Robin looked over at
the rock.

But it had moved!

Now it was in the darkest corner
of the room.

And it was shaking and moaning!

Christopher Robin crept toward the rock.

"B-b-be careful," warned Piglet.

Christopher Robin reached out

to touch the rock.

It was soft!

This wasn't a rock.

It was a blanket.

Christopher Robin lifted the blanket,

and underneath it was Eeyore!

"I was taking a nap,"

said Eeyore, "when I heard

all these scary noises.

So I hid in the corner."

Christopher Robin started to laugh.

"Eeyore," he said,

"you were afraid of yourself!"

"Oh my," said Eeyore.

"Isn't that silly."

"Well," said Christopher Robin,

"now that no one is afraid anymore,

let the Halloween parade begin!"

Everyone stepped outside.

And as they marched

through the Hundred-Acre Wood,

no one was afraid.

Well, maybe just a little bit.

Can you match the words with the pictures?

hat

honeypot

stripes

alphabet

ghost

Fill in the missing letters.

nur_e

O_l

ro_k

b_t

Eeyo_e